ᴅＩSNEY
POCAHONTAS

Ladybird

The English sailing ship, the *Susan Constant*, was nearly ready to sail. She was setting out from London on a voyage to the New World – America.

On the dockside, sailors were saying goodbye to their families. One sailor stood alone on the deck looking out to sea. He was Captain John Smith, a brave explorer who was eager to begin this new adventure.

At last, John Ratcliffe, the cruel and greedy man who was to govern the new colony in America, boarded the ship. He was followed by his faithful manservant, Wiggins, who was carrying Ratcliffe's pampered pug dog, Percy.

Far away in the New World, a young Indian girl stood on top of a cliff. She was Pocahontas, the brave and free-spirited daughter of Chief Powhatan. As always, her two companions were by her side – a playful raccoon called Meeko, and a protective hummingbird called Flit.

Suddenly, a voice called out from the river below. It was Pocahontas' best friend, Nakoma, in a canoe.

"Come home!" Nakoma cried. "Your father and the warriors have returned!"

With a graceful leap, Pocahontas dived smoothly into the water with Meeko and Flit not far behind. Soon, Pocahontas and Nakoma were paddling their way back to the Indian village.

At the Indian village Pocahontas heard Chief Powhatan announce that his warriors had been victorious in a battle with an enemy tribe. The villagers greeted the news happily.

As soon as Pocahontas was alone with her father she told him about a strange dream she had been having. "It makes me feel that something exciting is about to happen," she said.

Chief Powhatan smiled. "Something exciting *is* about to happen," he told her. "Kocoum has asked for your hand in marriage."

Pocahontas was shocked. Kocoum was a brave, handsome warrior – but he was so... *serious!* She certainly couldn't imagine herself married to him.

Then Chief Powhatan placed a beautiful necklace round Pocahontas' neck. "Your mother wore this at our wedding," he told her. "I hope you will wear it at yours."

Pocahontas was confused. How could she obey her father's wishes and marry Kocoum but still follow her own heart? She went to a special place in the forest, an enchanted glade, where she could talk with the wise, ancient tree spirit, Grandmother Willow.

"In my dream," Pocahontas told Grandmother Willow, "I see a spinning arrow. What can it mean?"

"I think this arrow is showing you your path in life," said Grandmother Willow. "Listen to the spirits all around you – in the earth, the water and the sky. Listen with your heart and these spirits will guide you down the right path."

Just then, Pocahontas felt a breeze ruffling her hair. She climbed up into Grandmother Willow's branches to hear what the wind was telling her.

In the distance, Pocahontas saw strange white clouds. She scrambled onto a rock to get a better view.

The clouds were really the sails of the *Susan Constant*, which soon dropped anchor off the coast. From her hiding place, Pocahontas saw a man come ashore to explore the forest. As the stranger came closer, Meeko ran over to greet him.

"Well, you're a strange-looking fellow!" said Smith, reaching into his leather pouch for a biscuit. He offered the treat to Meeko, who gobbled it up eagerly.

Just then, a bugle call came from the ship and Smith hurried back. He had not seen Pocahontas – yet.

Later that day, Governor Ratcliffe placed a flag in the ground. "I hereby claim this land for His Majesty, King James," he announced to the settlers. And to himself he said, "I'll claim all the gold we find here for *myself*!"

Meanwhile back at the Indian village, the warriors were discussing the arrival of the visitors. Chief Powhatan asked the wise medicine man, Kekata, what he could learn about them.

Kekata threw some powder into a fire and studied the terrible wolf shapes that rose out of the smoke. "These men consume everything in their path," he said. "Their weapons spout fire and thunder!"

Chief Powhatan was worried by what he had heard. He told Kocoum and some other warriors to keep an eye on the newcomers. "Let us hope they do not intend to stay long," he said.

Governor Ratcliffe didn't want anyone to get in the way of his plans to become rich so he sent Smith back into the forest to scout for Indians.

As Smith explored the new land, he came to a sparkling waterfall. It was here that Smith saw Pocahontas for the first time. The moment their eyes met, their lives were changed forever.

"Wait, please!" called Smith, as Pocahontas darted off towards her canoe. "I won't hurt you."

A breeze swirled around Pocahontas and she remembered Grandmother Willow's advice to listen to the spirits. She let the handsome stranger take her hand and help her out of her canoe.

As their hands touched, Pocahontas and Smith knew they were falling in love.

Meanwhile, the settlers were digging for gold. They chopped down trees and hacked at the earth with their spades, scarring the landscape.

Hidden in some bushes, Kocoum and another warrior, Namontack, watched as their land was destroyed.

Wiggins threw a drumstick into the bushes and Percy raced in after it. When the dog saw Namontack he yelped in surprise and the settlers ran for their guns.

A terrible fight followed and Namontack was shot and wounded. When Chief Powhatan learned what had happened he warned his people to stay away from the settlers.

Deep in the forest, Smith and Pocahontas had learned each other's names and Pocahontas was teaching Smith how to say 'hello' in her language.

While the two talked, Meeko searched through Smith's pouch looking for food. He found Smith's compass and, thinking it was a biscuit, ran off with it and hid it in a nearby tree.

Pocahontas told Smith about her people's beliefs. "To us, all of nature is one," she said. "The earth, plants, animals, people, even the wind and the sky are all connected."

As Pocahontas spoke, Smith realised that the Indians were not savages as he and the other settlers had thought. Instead, they were a proud people who lived in harmony with the land.

Next morning, Pocahontas and Nakoma were gathering corn in a field when Smith appeared. "I had to see you again," he told Pocahontas.

Nakoma couldn't believe that Pocahontas was talking to one of their enemies! "Please don't say anything," Pocahontas begged Nakoma as she took Smith's hand and walked with him into the forest.

Pocahontas led Smith to the enchanted glade where she introduced him to Grandmother Willow.

Before Smith left, he and Pocahontas agreed to meet in the enchanted glade again that night. "It seems to me you have found your path," said Grandmother Willow to Pocahontas.

Back at the Indian village, Pocahontas found the warriors preparing for battle with the settlers.

"Isn't there another way, Father?" she asked. "Can't you talk to the settlers instead of fighting them?"

"They do not want to talk," said Chief Powhatan.

*　*　*

Back at the settlers' camp, Governor Ratcliffe was in a rage because his men hadn't found any gold. "Those savages are hiding it all!" he shouted.

"The Indians aren't savages," Smith protested, "and they're not hiding anything. The only gold they have is golden food," he said, showing Ratcliffe an ear of corn that Pocahontas had given him.

"Lies! Lies!" thundered Ratcliffe. "This is *my* land and *I* make the laws! I say we have to kill the Indians!"

Later that night, Smith and Pocahontas secretly met in the enchanted glade. Pocahontas begged Smith to talk to her father and try to stop the battle.

When Smith agreed, she hugged him happily. As they embraced, the two shared a tender kiss.

Suddenly, someone burst from the bushes. It was Kocoum, who had secretly followed Pocahontas into the forest. As he lunged at Smith, a young settler named Thomas appeared. He fired his gun at Kocoum and the brave warrior fell to the ground, dead.

Smith told Thomas to run as Pocahontas rushed over to where Kocoum's body lay.

Then, as Pocahontas watched in horror, a party of warriors led Smith away. They took him to Chief Powhatan, saying he was responsible for Kocoum's death. The Chief declared that Smith must die at sunrise.

Heartbroken and confused, Pocahontas went back to the enchanted glade. "Everything's gone wrong," she told Grandmother Willow. "I feel so lost."

Just then, Meeko brought Pocahontas something – it was Smith's compass, which he had retrieved from its hiding place in the tree. As Pocahontas gazed at it the needle began to spin. When it stopped, it was pointing towards the rising sun.

"The spinning arrow from my dream!" she exclaimed. "It's showing me my path! I must get back before it's too late!" Swift as the wind, Pocahontas sped back towards her village.

As Chief Powhatan raised his club to kill Smith, Pocahontas raced past him and threw herself over Smith's body to protect him.

"If you kill him, you'll have to kill me too!" she cried. "Look around you, Father, and see where the path of hatred has brought us!"

Chief Powhatan looked at his warriors on one side and the settlers on the other. "My daughter speaks the truth," he said at last. "Let us be guided to a path of peace."

As the Indians lowered their weapons, Ratcliffe saw his chance. "Fire!" he ordered his men. But the settlers now saw how greedy and selfish Ratcliffe was and they also lowered their weapons.

Ratcliffe grabbed a gun and fired at Chief Powhatan himself. Smith leapt in front of the Chief and the bullet hit him instead.

The furious settlers grabbed Ratcliffe, bound him in chains and took him back to the *Susan Constant*.

A few days later, John Smith lay on a stretcher ready for his trip back to England. Pocahontas knelt beside him with tears in her eyes.

"Come with me," Smith begged her.

Pocahontas looked up. Nearby, Indians were sharing their food with the hungry settlers. For the first time, there was peace between the two sides. Pocahontas knew at last what her true path was – she told Smith she had to stay and help keep the new peace alive.

"Then I'll stay here with you," Smith said.

"No," said Pocahontas. "You have to go home if you are to survive. But no matter what happens, I will always be with you – forever."

Pocahontas kept that thought in her heart as she stood on the cliff top watching the *Susan Constant* carry her beloved John Smith away across the sea.

Ladybird books are widely available, but in case of difficulty may be ordered by post or telephone from:
Ladybird Books – Cash Sales Department Littlegate Road Paignton Devon TQ3 3BE Telephone 01803 554761

A catalogue record for this book is available from the British Library

Published by Ladybird Books Ltd Loughborough Leicestershire UK
LADYBIRD and the device of a Ladybird are trademarks of Ladybird Books Ltd